WHOOzoo at the Zoo

By Chet Fanning *with illustrations by Rick Reed*

The Pachyderm's nose

Is just like a hose.

It gives him the knack

To sprinkle his back

And helps him to wash his big toes.

He avoids his Mom's wrath

With a once-a-day bath.

Now see how his epiderm' glows.

3

A diet of chewy bamboo

A Panda's delighted to chew.

It's not on my diet.

I'd rather not try it,

But a Panda will chew till he's through.

He'll rarely go play

'Cause he sits there all day

Making his tasty 'boo stew.

4

5

You can tell by the roar

That there's trouble in store.

For the princely Lion

Is actually tryin'

To give you "What For."

He yawns quite a lot,

But it's tired he's not.

You'll know when he's sleeping; he'll snore

6

7

The Giraffe is so tall and so stately.

Have you seen one in your neighborhood late

He's blessed with a heck

Of a long, skinny neck,

So over everything else he stands greatly.

But sometimes, I fear,

If you track him too near,

He will look at you rather irately.

8

9

Have you noticed a Grizzly Bear's paws?

They're huge and have giant, sharp claws.

All to help it climb high,

Nearly up to the sky,

And give its predators pause.

Momma gives it a boost

To where it can roost,

And for that she deserves our applause.

10

11

The teeth of a Beaver

Are sharp as a cleaver.

He will chew down some trees,

His Daddy to please,

Doing work in a veritable fever.

A strong home must be had

So he's coached by his Dad,

And now he's a master log weaver.

13

The Hippo's a gigantic lump

From his nose clear back to his rump.

He gets mad when it's hot.

He gets mad when it's not.

So he just sits down with a thump.

Then he stands in the pool

Just to get himself cool,

And it keeps him from being a grump.

14

Consider the unique Kangaroo
From the land of the didgeridoo.
With kids in her pocket,
She's off like a rocket.
It would be perfectly great if she flew.
She hops over the land
And right over the sand,
But when she tries swimming, she's through!

16

17

See that cute little Leopard?

Has she been salted and peppered?

Her body is covered with spots

And so are those of her tots.

So she can hide them away like a shepherd.

She snuggles them up,

Then gets them their "sup,"

'Cause Moms keep their kids out of jeopard

19

A Rhinoceros's horn

Is sharp as a thorn.

When used as a spear,

It's something to fear.

But it's only the way he was born.

It's really just hair

That's put there to scare.

Just be careful your pants don't get torn.

20

21

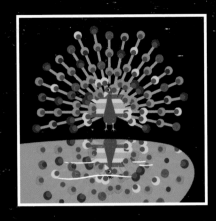

The Peacock has marvelous flair,

Because brilliant feathers are there.

He swishes aroun'

All over the town,

Just to make everyone stare.

He struts all about

While his tail feathers sprout

As he tries to be one of a pair.

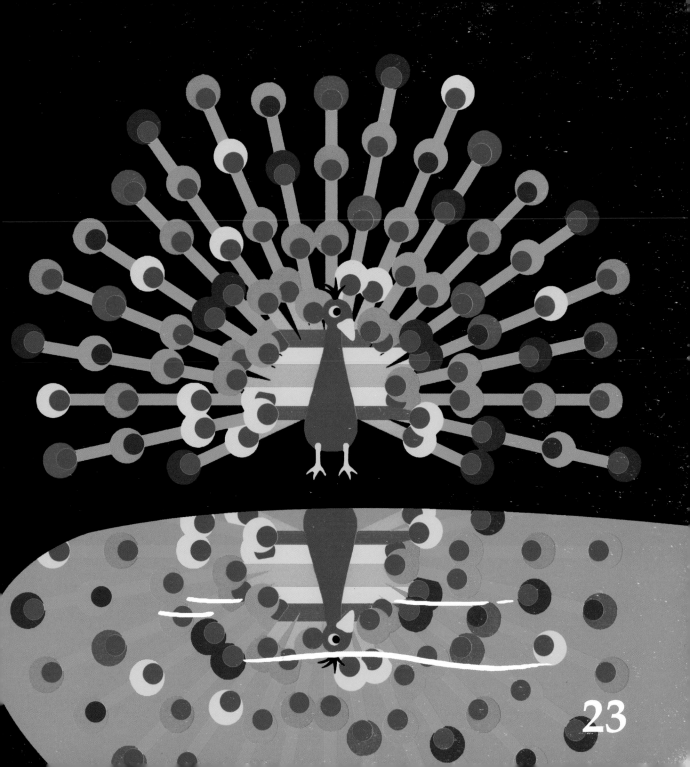

23

On long, skinny legs she will stand

Way up to her neck in the sand.

Is this some technique

To play hide-and-seek?

No, this Mom has something else planned.

Dad dug a large hole

To store eggs down below.

What teamwork! Why, isn't that grand?

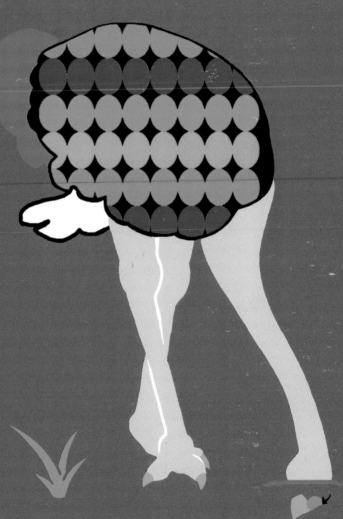

The Tiger's a really big cat,

But I'm sure you already know that.

Its kittens will purr

When you pet on their fur.

They'll sit snug in your arms and lie flat.

But Dad's got a great growl,

When he's in a mood foul.

So don't count on him for a chat.

27

The fleece of the popular Llamas

Makes extra soft, cozy pajamas.

But their coat's even better

When made into a sweater.

And it really pleases their Mamas.

But these sweet little guys

Will spit in your eyes

If they think you are going to cause traumas

29

While he howls at the moon

He likes to think it's a croon.

He's telling his mate,

"Don't you be late.

I'm expecting you over here soon."

But when back in the den,

Just like all other men,

Mr. Wolf sings a different tune.

30

31

Add pretty colors. Use them ever so clever.
And this book is then yours for ever and ever.

This book belongs to _____

Age _____ **Date** _____

**This book was
given to me by** _____

My signature _____